GONE CAMPING

A Novel in Verse

By Tamera Will Wissinger

Illustrated by Matthew Cordell

Houghton Mifflin Harcourt

BOSTON NEW YORK

The text of this book is set in Bodoni, ScalaSans, Kidprint, and Palatino. The illustrations are pen and ink with watercolor.

Library of Congress Cataloging-in-Publication Data
Names: Wissinger, Tamera Will, author.
Title: Gone camping / by Tamera Will Wissinger.
Description: Boston : Houghton Mifflin Harcourt, [2017] | Summary: "Camping is fun. Until it's time to sleep. Then, Lucy wonders, what kinds of creatures lurk in the dark? With only her brother and grandpa as tent mates, will Lucy be able to face her camping fears? Includes a variety of poetic forms — from aubade to haiku — as well as writing tips about rhyme and rhythm." — Provided by publisher. | Includes bibliographical references.
Identifiers: LCCN 2016014201 | ISBN 9780544638730 (hardcover)
Subjects: | CYAC: Novels in verse. | Camping — Fiction. | Nature — Fiction. | Brothers and sisters — Fiction. | Grandfathers — Fiction. | BISAC: JUVENILE FICTION / Stories in Verse. | JUVENILE FICTION / Sports & Recreation / Camping & Outdoor Activities. | JUVENILE FICTION / Family / Multigenerational. | JUVENILE FICTION / Family / Siblings. | JUVENILE FICTION / Nature & the Natural World / Environment.
Classification: LCC PZ7.5.W57 Gm 2017 | DDC [Fic] — dc23
LC record available at https://lccn.loc.gov/2016014201

Manufactured in the United States of America
DOC 10 9 8 7 6 5 4 3 2
4500658703

For Pete, who listens to my writing dreams
and helps me make them come true.
With love, T.W.W.

To Romy and Dean,
my very own Lucy and Sam.
M.C.

CNTENTS

Sam

PROVISIONING
Tercet Variation

Late night.
House bright.
Everybody packs tonight.

Summer: Here.
Trip: Near.
Mom and Lucy check our gear.

Map out.
Plan our route.
Dad named me chief camp scout.

One more
Final chore.
Duffel mountain near the door.

Next day.
No delay.
Campsite: We are on our way!

PACKING LIST
List Poem

√   Tent
√   Poles
√   Stakes
√   Hammer
√   Rope

√   Grill kit
√   Food
√   Bucket
√   Soap

√   Sleeping bags
√   Canoe
√   Canteen

√   Lantern
√   Duffel bags
√   Sunscreen

√   Fishing gear
√   First-aid kit

√   Four campers
√   One car
√   Tight fit

Sam and Lucy

GOING CAMPING
Dramatic Poem for Two

Sam	Lucy

Sam

We'll set up camp,
Go hiking,
Catch our bait.

Lucy

We'll build a blazing fire,
Stay up late.

Sam

We'll cool off by the lake.
We'll barbecue.

Lucy

We'll fish with Mom and Dad
In our canoe.

Sam

Tomorrow's almost here.
Hooray!

Lucy

Hooray!
We're going camping in a day!

NIGHTTIME CRITTERS
Confessional Poem

Camping in the tent sounds fun—
Until it's time to sleep.
That's when nighttime critters chatter,
Shadows twist and creep.

The tent is one big room
Without a single place to hide,
But Mom and Dad will save us
If a critter crawls inside.

Sam and Lucy

SHAKE AWAKE
Dramatic Poem for Two

Sam	*Lucy*

Sam: Jump UP! Shake awake.

Lucy: Let's head to the lake.

Sam: We're ready to go.

Lucy: No time to be slow.

Sam: The sun's about to rise.

Lucy: We made breakfast, too—

Sam: Surprise!

Lucy: Surprise!

Dad, Lucy, and Sam

CHANGE OF PLANS
Dramatic Poem for Three

Dad	Lucy	Sam

Hachoo! Hachoo!

What's that? A sneeze?

Hachoo! Hachoo!
Ha-CHOO!

Who's sneezing—
Is it allergies?

Hachoo! Hachoo!
It's be, kids.
I'b too sick to camp.
I deed to stay id bed.
Bob will stay with be
Ad Gramp
will go with you idstead.

Lucy

A TRICK

Lament

This must be a trick.
Dad is never ever sick.

The tent, no Mom? No fair!
We won't be *safe* without her there.

Say it isn't true.
We won't go camping without you two.

Sam

SUPER DUPER
Cinquain

Although
Dad didn't mean
to be—turns out he's a
super duper camping party
pooper.

GOOD TO GO
Counting Poem

One. Two.
So much to do.
Where'd I leave my other shoe?

Three. Four.
Behind the door.
They've never asked *me* to camp before.

Five. Six.
Fiddlesticks!
I'm almost out of candy mix.

Seven. Eight.
I'm running late.
I don't want to make them wait.

Nine. Ten.
I'm done—amen.
I'm good to go, kids; just say when!

Lucy

BE BRAVE, LUCY
Confidence Poem

I really wanted Mom along—
I'd feel safer with her nearby.

But leaving Dad alone is wrong.
Be brave, Lucy—
                    At least you can try.

Sam

GRANDPA–PROS AND CONS
Fourteener

I don't think Grandpa's ever fished, canoed, or camped before.
He putters, owns a radio, and rarely goes outdoors.

But Grandpa's funny, shares his candy, drives, can barbecue.
Maybe we'll still have fun without Mom, Dad, or the canoe?

Lucy

THE WOODS AHEAD
Rondelet

In the woods ahead
Branches and shadows reach everywhere.
In the woods ahead
How will I ever go to bed?
Who knows what creatures lurk in there.
Could be raccoons, or fox, or bear
In the woods ahead.

Sam

CAMP AHOY
Couplets

Look! The campground Welcome sign.
Water—see it shimmer-shine?

Our campsite's just around the bend.
Take this road to the very end.

Let's park and we'll unload our gear.
Camp ahoy—yippee! We're *here.*

Sam

TENT PITCHING
How-To Poem

Choose a site that's flat and high.
Over here it's smooth and dry.

Stand the poles straight base to top.
Careful, Gramp—don't let it flop.

Grip the stakes, pound them tight.
Good job, Lucy. Use your might.

Tie the flaps open wide,
Scrunch down low, crawl inside.

Our tent stands strong by an old oak tree.
A sturdy canvas cave for three.

Lucy

THE WALLS OF OUR TENT
Quatrain

During the day the tent is bright.
How dark will it get tonight?
The walls of our tent are flimsy-thin.
Could something wild wiggle right in?

Lucy

IF A CRITTER CREEPS IN
What-If Poem

What if a snake slithers up from the shore?
What if a mudpuppy slips through our door?

What if a bat flutters onto my nose?
What if a crawdaddy pinches my toes?

What if a field mouse nips at my ear?
What if a smelly skunk sprays in here?

What if I freeze 'cause I'm too scared to shout?
        If a critter creeps in—
What if *I* can't get out?

Lucy

SLEEPING BAG CHARM
Charm Poem

Sleeping bag, sleeping bag,
Soft and snug.
Sleeping bag, sleeping bag,
Like a hug.
Sleeping bag—be my
Safe cocoon.
Sleeping bag, sleeping bag,
See you soon.

Sam and Lucy

FOLLOW THE TRAIL
Rondel

Sam   *Lucy*

One by one let's follow the trail.

                    Hike—Two—Three—Four.

Down to the lake—we're going to explore.

                    Hurdle the puddle and tiny snail.

Under the thicket—a covey of quail

Scratch for seeds on the forest floor.

                    One by one let's follow the trail.

Hike—Two—Three—Four.

                    Nesting beaver flaps her tail.

Osprey searches, plunges, soars.

Camp is this way—around the shore.

                    Bye, little boat with the puffy sail.

One by one let's follow the trail.

Hike—Two—Three—Four.   Hike—Two—Three—Four.

BAIT CATCHERS
How-To Poem

Everybody take a jar.
We're losing daylight—there's a star.

Look for different kinds of bugs,
Spiders, worms, or even slugs.

They'll scatter if we hesitate.
Go quickly, team: Let's catch our bait.

Sam

HOW TO BUILD A BONFIRE
Narrative Poem

Set

Stones in a circle

On clean open ground. Scatter

Sticks, tiny twigs in the round. Lay long-

Legged logs like a great pyramid. Tuck leaves

In layers by the twigs. Strike a match on a stone, wake a

Single small spark. Light leaves, stand back: eclipse the dark.

Lucy

SONG OF THE BEANIE WEENIE BARBECUE
Chant

Queenie, queenie: boil the beanies,
Fire, burn and roast the weenies.

Sliced-up bits of footlong dogs,
In the cauldron on these logs;
Eye of onion, ketchup squirt,
Dark brown sugar, mustard spurt,
Stir the pot of beans and pork,
Taste it with a camping spork.
For a gruel of powerful beanies,
In the cauldron roast the weenies.

Queenie, queenie: boil the beanies,
Fire, burn and roast the weenies.

Cool it till there's no more bubble,
Come and get it—on the double!

Sam

RULES FOR EATING S'MORES
Limerick

Eating s'mores is a blast, but it's tricky.
S'mores won't let you be tidy or picky.
You can slurp, chomp, or lick,
Nibble slow, gobble quick.
Makes no difference—you're going to get sticky.

Lucy

FOREST GLOW
Haiku

Let the fire burn.
Let it brighten to the moon.
Darkness came too soon.

45

Lucy

TWINKLE, TWINKLE, MIGHTY MARS
Wish Poem

Twinkle, Twinkle, Mighty Mars,
In the sky among the stars.

Ruby planet, bold and bright,
Here's my wish this camping night:

Let me be alert and strong.
And keep the bears where they belong.

.

Sam

DOUSING THE FIRE
Concrete Poem

Water Trickles, Dribbles, Drizzles, Hisses,

Sputters, Crackles, Sizzles. Fire

Withers, Weakens,

fizzles.

Lucy

BY LANTERN LIGHT
Free Verse Poem

The trail to the washroom seems

N
A
R
R
O
W

A
S

A

T
W
I
G

And when an owl

"Whooo! Whooo! Whooot!"s

We nearly jump out of our boots.

Grandpa

STICK TOGETHER
Octave

Stick together on the trail.
Sam—you bring up the rear.
Lucy, hold my hand.
If we're a train, I'm engineer.

The air feels gummy—like Super Glue.
Could be a change of weather.
Here's the washroom. Clean up quickly, team.
And stick together.

Grandpa

BEDTIME BLESSING
Blessing Poem

Here's a gumdrop before bed tonight—
You'll taste too good for boogeyman's bite.
See you when the sun shines bright.
Good night.
Sweet dreams.
Sleep tight.

Lucy

TO NOISES IN THE NIGHT
Poem of Address

Spookiness, Shadows, Strange Noises: Beware.
I'm not so little or easy to scare.

Spookiness, Shadows, Strange Noises: Behave.
I am ferocious: I'm Lucy the Brave.

My shield is this pillow—my sword, this flashlight.
Spookiness, Shadows, Strange Noises: *GOOD NIGHT.*

Lucy

OPPOSITE OF CREEPY
Opposite Poem

What is the opposite of creepy?

Tummy full,

snuggled in,

and

feeling

very

sleepy.

TENT MATES
Quatrain

My grandpa said, "Go to sleep quickly."
My grandpa said, "Have a sweet dream."
My grandpa neglected to mention:
He snores like a **train full of steam.**

Lucy and Sam

BEWARE
Alarm Poem

Lucy	Sam

Grandpa!
Sam!
Beware—
A BEAR!
He's in our tent!
Hear him ROAR?
The door is over here—Come quick!

Lucy,
That's nothing more
Than Grandpa's snore.

Lucy

WOODLAND MIDNIGHT BAND
Serenade

Knee-Deep

Knee-Deep

Tick-a

Tick-a

Tink

Creek-a

Creek-a

Chip

Chip

Wish

Wash

Wink.

Knee-Deep Knee-Deep—

I know that sound.

Knee Deep

Knee Deep

Tick-a
Tick-a
Tink

Creek-a
Creek-a
Chip

Wish
wash
wink

That's a frog by the lake
Squatted low to the ground.

Tick-a tick-a tink—
That's branches in a tree.
Creek-a creek-a chip—
That's a cricket family.

Wish wash wink—
That's water at the shore.
I know these sounds.
I've heard them all before.

Knee-deep

Knee-deep

Tick-a

Tick-a

Tink

Creek-a

Creek-a

Chip

Chip

Wish

Wash

Wink.

Lucy

BEDTIME IN THE FOREST
Fill-in-the-Blank Poem

Bullfrog's song has faded,
Not one cricket makes a cheep.
Maybe all the forest families

                 finally

                    fell

                         _____.

                      Answer: asleep

Lucy

GOODBYE, LAST NIGHT
Aubade

Little light, a little lighter.
Bit of bright, now burning brighter.
Dark is shifting—drifting away.
Goodbye, last night. Hello, today.

Did it rain? The forest is glimmering.
Leaves and pine needles are shimmering.
How lucky to see the sun's first ray.
Goodbye, last night. Hello, today.

Lucy

SHADOWS CAN'T GRAB
Epiphany

I stayed very still and I listened last night—
The woods clatter-chattered and rattled, all right.
It can *be* spooky outside with no light,
But shadows can't grab and strange noises don't bite.

Lucy and Grandpa

WAKE-UP CALL
Dramatic Poem for Two

Lucy   *Grandpa*

Grandpa? Sam? You're missing daybreak.
Sleepyheads—are you awake?

                       It's so early, Lucy, dear.

The fish are up—they're jumping, hear?
We'll catch a bunch, I bet.

                       Okay.
                       I'll grab the net.

Lucy, Sam and Grandpa

FISHING FRENZY!
Tongue Twister

Lucy	Sam	Grandpa

It's a frenzy—
fishing frenzy!
Fish are everywhere
we look.

Lucy	Sam
It's a frenzy— fishing frenzy!	It's a frenzy— fishing frenzy! Fish are fighting for my hook.

Lucy	Sam	Grandpa
It's a frenzy— fishing frenzy!	It's a frenzy— fishing frenzy!	It's a frenzy— fishing frenzy! Caught our limit— we are through!

What a frenzy—
fishing frenzy!   Fishing frenzy!   Fishing frenzy!

Finest

                       Fishing

                                              Frenzy

WHEW!   WHEW!   WHEW!

Lucy

FISHING SKILLS
Quatrain

Wait till we tell Mom and Dad how many fish we caught.
Wait till Dad hears all about our fishing frenzy spot.
Wait till I show Mom my mighty fighting arm.
Wait till we tell Dad that Gramp's our lucky fishing charm.

Sam

SHORE BREAKFAST
Sestet

Fish grilled over wood
Smells smoky good.
Best breakfast by the shore.

Mm. Mm. Yum.
Fish in my tum.
Eat up—there's plenty more.

Lucy

RACE TO THE LAKE
Pun Poem

How can we leave?
Camping's so much fun.

We *have* to swim
Before we're done.

Race you, Grandpa.
Three,
Two,
RUN!

83

Lucy, Sam, and Grandpa

CANNON BALL!
Concrete Poem

TAKE OFF

CURL SMALL

FLY HIGH

F
A
S
T

F
A
L
L

SPLASH DOWN

CANNON BALL!

Lucy

TEAR DOWN
Reprise poem

Midday.
Can't stay.
Tear-down time at camp today.

Duffels: Stacked.
Tent: Slacked.
All our gear is tightly packed.

Lakeshore.
Encore.
One last look, then shut the door.

Map out.
Reverse route.
Sam says this time *I'll* be scout.

Lucy

MY FAVORITE PARTS OF CAMPING
Letter Poem

Dear Mom and Dad—

We pitched our tent, explored the trail, captured bait in jars.
I cooked our beanie-weenies and was first to notice Mars.
I thought I heard a bear, but it was only Grandpa's snore.
Sleeping in the tent at night won't scare *me* anymore.
We filled our stringers, cannonballed when I said, "Three, Two, Run."
We stuck together always—one for three and three for one.

Can we go back next weekend? I really love to camp.
And this time can we *all* go? Mom and me, Dad, Sam, *and* Gramp?

Love, Lucy

PROVISIONING FOR POETRY

Just as Lucy and Sam used provisions on their camping trip, poets have provisions for writing poetry. The poet's provisions include rhythm, rhyme, poetry techniques, stanzas, and poetic forms.

In this section, you'll find poetry provision details that I hope will help you with your poetry writing.

In camping and in writing, I wish you well.

— Tamera

RHYME

Rhyme is two or more words with endings that sound exactly alike. Here are some rhyming basics:

- Pairing words with one syllable each, like CAMP and GRAMP, is probably the simplest way to rhyme.
- When words have two syllables that rhyme with each other, that's called a double rhyme. DRIZZLE and SIZZLE is a double rhyme, because the first syllables—DRIZ and SIZ—rhyme, and so do the second syllables. Double rhymes can also be made using combinations of one and two syllable words, like SKIP GO and TIPTOE.
- Rhymes are usually found at the ends of sentences and are called end rhyme. Sometimes, though, poets use rhyming words in the middle of the lines. That's called internal rhyme.
- Words don't have to be spelled the same way to work as a rhyme. BITE and BRIGHT rhyme just as well as NIGHT and BRIGHT.
- Sometimes words that are spelled alike, like DO and SO, look like they should rhyme, but they don't. That's called eye rhyme.
- Some poetic forms call for specific rhyming patterns. Other forms don't have to include any rhyming words at all.

RHYTHM

Rhythm is the tempo or the beat of a poem. Poets create rhythm by choosing each word carefully. They notice syllables and where the emphasis within words and phrases naturally falls. They consider how words sound alone and when they are combined on the page with other words. How long or short lines are is another rhythm choice poets make. Creating strong rhythm is an important job—it helps give your poems energy and gives your readers clues about how to read your poems.

Rhythm Patterns Come from Syllable Combinations

- There are four common rhythm patterns. Two patterns are based on pairs of syllables, and two are based on groupings of three syllables.
- In the poem "Tent Pitching," the two-syllable **trochaic** rhythm begins with a strong beat and is followed by an unstressed one: "CHOOSE a / SITE that's / FLAT and / HIGH." Hear the extra stressed syllable at the end of the line? That's common with trochaic rhythm.
- The two-syllable **iambic** rhythm in "Grandpa—Pros and Cons" has this pattern: "i DON'T / think GRAND / pa's EV / er FISHED, / caNOED, / or CAMPED / beFORE." This time, the strong beat is on the second syllable in each pair, and the first is unstressed.
- "To Noises in the Night" has a good example of a strong three-syllable rhythm with one stressed beat followed by two unstressed ones—this is called **dactylic** rhythm: "SPOOKiness / SHADows, strange / NOISes: be / WARE." There is an extra syllable at the end of this line, too. That extra stressed beat bridges each line so that it sounds natural.
- Here is the three-syllable **anapestic** rhythm in "Tent Mates": "My GRAND / pa said, 'GO / to sleep QUICK / ly.'" With two unstressed beats followed by one stressed beat, this rhythm is

the opposite of dactylic rhythm. Notice how there is only one unstressed beat at the beginning and another at the end? Little variations like that are not unusual with anapestic rhythm and help the poem flow smoothly.

Line Lengths Come from Rhythm Pattern Combinations

- In rhythm, line length is the partner to syllables. Once you know which syllables are stressed in each line, you can count those.
- One set of stressed and unstressed syllables is called a foot or meter.
- The examples from "Tent Pitching" and "To Noises in the Night" have four accented syllables, so four feet. Even when there is only a partial foot, it counts if the syllable is stressed.
- "Grandpa—Pros and Cons" has seven feet per line. The line from "Tent Mates" has three feet.
- Lines in poetry can be any length you choose unless you are following a poetic form—and even then, you can make exceptions.

POETRY TECHNIQUES

Poetry techniques are special word or phrase choices. Using them well can help make poems interesting and exciting to readers.

ALLITERATION

Alliteration happens when the poet uses two or more words close together that begin with the same sound. In the poem "Bedtime in the Forest," "forest families finally fell" is an example of alliteration. Alliterative words can also be found in "Dousing the Fire," "Goodbye, Last Night," and "Fishing Frenzy."

ANAPHORA

Anaphora is when the poet starts several lines of a poem with the same word or phrase. It's useful for drawing attention to something or emphasizing an emotion. The phrase *What if* starts most of the lines in "If a Critter Creeps In." It shows Lucy's worry about woodland creatures sneaking into the tent. "To Noises in the Night" and "Fishing Skills" also have anaphora phrases.

APOSTROPHE
Apostrophe lets the speaker in a poem talk to a person, an animal, or a thing that can't reply. In the poem "To Noises in the Night," when Lucy says, "Spookiness, Shadows, Strange Noises: Beware," that is apostrophe. "Sleeping Bag Charm," "Twinkle, Twinkle, Mighty Mars," and "Goodbye, Last Night" also use apostrophe.

ASSONANCE
With assonance, the poet repeats a vowel sound within some words in a poem. This is sometimes called vowel rhyme, although it might be used in words that do or don't rhyme. The short *i* sound in the words *trickles, dribbles,* and *drizzles* are a few of the examples of assonance in the poem "Dousing the Fire."

HYPERBOLE
Hyperbole lets the poet exaggerate the truth to help draw attention to a situation. In "Fishing Frenzy," hyperbole is in the line "Fish are everywhere we look." Fish really aren't everywhere, but that overstatement helps make the point that there are many fish in the lake. "By Lantern Light" also has a line of hyperbole.

IMAGERY
Imagery is a way for the poet to use touch, taste, sight, sound, or smell to help the reader imagine what's happening. In the poem "Goodbye, Last Night," there are examples of imagery in the lines "The forest is glimmering./Leaves and pine needles are shimmering." "Camp Ahoy," "Stick Together," "How to Build a Bonfire," "Dousing the Fire," and "Shore Breakfast" also include strong imagery.

INTERJECTION

An interjection is a word or phrase that shows a burst of emotion. It can be used to display a speaker's mood—good or bad. In "Going Camping," Lucy and Sam shout, "Hooray!" That one word shows how excited they are about their trip. "Camp Ahoy" also includes an interjection.

METAPHOR

A metaphor is a figure of speech that lets the poet connect two different things to make a point. Metaphors don't have to be based on facts. Stretching the truth brings an idea into sharper focus so the reader is sure to pay attention. In "Tent Pitching," Sam calls the tent "a sturdy canvas cave." By comparing the tent to a cave, Sam shows that he is confident in how they built it. "Provisioning" also has a metaphor.

ONOMATOPOEIA

Onomatopoeia is a word or phrase that lets the poet imitate a real sound. In "Rules for Eating S'mores," all of the eating noises—*slurp, chomp, lick, nibble,* and *gobble*—are onomatopoeia. "Change of Plans," "Dousing the Fire," "By Lantern Light," "Woodland Midnight Band," and "Shadows Can't Grab" also have onomatopoetic words and phrases.

PERSONIFICATION

Personification lets poets pretend that things or animals are human-like. "Sleeping Bag Charm" and "Twinkle, Twinkle, Mighty Mars" are whole poems that use personification—they show Lucy talking to her sleeping bag and to Mars. Those are also poems of address. In "How to Build a Bonfire," "wake a single small spark" is one line of personification within a narrative poem. Waking up is something normally done by a person or animal, not by a spark of fire.

REFRAIN

A refrain is a line or lines in a poem that show up more than once. It can stand alone or be part of a stanza. "Follow the Trail" has a refrain that is part of the rondel form, which includes these lines that repeat at the start, middle, and end of the poem: "One by one let's follow the trail./ Hike–Two–Three–Four." "Sleeping Bag Charm," "Song of the Beanie Weenie Barbecue," "Goodbye, Last Night," and "Woodland Midnight Band" also have refrains.

SIMILE

A simile is a way to describe something using the words *like* or *as.* To create a simile, the poet makes a comparison between two things that may not seem to be alike. It can be quite an exaggeration, as in this line from "Stick Together": "The air feels gummy–like Super Glue." The air doesn't really feel like Super Glue, but comparing these two things is an interesting way to say that the air feels humid and sticky. "Sleeping Bag Charm," "How to Build a Bonfire," "By Lantern Light," and "Tent Mates" each have a simile, too.

POETIC FORMS AND STANZA PATTERNS

Poetic forms and stanza patterns are used in a way similar to how Sam and Lucy use their road maps. Forms and stanzas help a poet move from the starting point of an idea to the ending point of a completed poem. Some forms and stanzas are quick and easy to follow, and others might take more time.

ALARM POEM

The job of an alarm poem is to alert someone to wake up or take action, just as an alarm would. In "Beware," Lucy acts as the alarm when she thinks she hears a bear in the tent. Alarm poems don't need to follow a specific rhythm or rhyme pattern.

AUBADE

An aubade features the sunrise and can be either joyful or sad. An aubade can rhyme, but it doesn't have to, and it can take any form. In "Goodbye, Last Night," Lucy is very happy to greet the sun as it rises. This poem is also a kyrielle.

BLANK VERSE VARIATION

Blank verse follows a rhythm pattern, but there isn't end rhyme. "How to Build a Bonfire" is a variation of a blank verse poem. The third and fourth lines don't have end rhyme. Instead, they follow the rhythm pattern set up in the first lines.

BLESSING POEM

A blessing poem lets the speaker give good wishes to someone or something. "Bedtime Blessing" is Grandpa's lighthearted way of telling Lucy and Sam good night. Blessing poems may or may not rhyme or follow a set pattern.

CHANT POEM

As the title "Song of the Beanie Weenie Barbecue" suggests, a chant poem is a type of song. Instead of being set to music, though, a chant poem has a strong, catchy rhythm that lets people join in. Chant poems may have first been used for religious ceremonies. Today chant poems can be about any topic and don't always rhyme.

CHARM POEM

A charm poem stems from wanting to make something better or to have a positive effect. A charm poem can be serious or upbeat and doesn't have to follow a set pattern. "Sleeping Bag Charm" is Lucy's cheerful way of trying to feel safe in the tent.

CINQUAIN

A cinquain is a stanza that has five lines. "Super Duper" is a cinquain that follows a twenty-two-syllable pattern created by the poet Adelaide Crapsey. Often the five lines form one long unrhymed sentence. The first line has two syllables, the second has four, then six, then eight, then back to two. "Rules for Eating S'mores" is a cinquain stanza of a different kind: It is a limerick.

CONCRETE POEM/SHAPE POEM

When a poet writes a poem in the shape of the topic, it's known as a concrete poem. A concrete poem could be about anything and may rhyme, but it doesn't have to. "Cannon Ball!" is a rhyming concrete poem. The words are rounded like a cannon ball (or a jumping swimmer). "How to Build a Bonfire" and "Dousing the Fire" are also poems that are shaped like their subjects.

CONFESSIONAL POEM

This form lets the speaker in the poem admit something. It could be about what someone did, feelings toward another person, or some other topic. In "Nighttime Critters," Lucy confesses her camping fear. A confessional poem doesn't have to rhyme or follow a special pattern.

CONFIDENCE POEM

A confidence poem is about determination or building up faith in someone. Lucy gives herself a pep talk in "Be Brave, Lucy." This form could also be written so the speaker is helping someone else. It can be any length and may or may not rhyme.

COUNTING POEM

In a counting poem, the speaker will count. It's up to the poet to decide which way to count, how high or low, and whether or not the poem will rhyme. It's not as simple as listing numbers, though. A counting poem needs a purpose. In "Good to Go" Grandpa counts while he quickly gets ready to go camping with Lucy and Sam.

COUPLET

A couplet is small—it has just two lines. Poets usually use couplets to build longer poems. "Camp Ahoy" is a six-line poem made with three couplet stanzas. "Grandpa—Pros and Cons" is an example of a poem with two sets of couplets that have long lines. Many times couplets rhyme, but they don't have to.

DRAMATIC POEM

In a dramatic poem, the speaker or speakers sound like they're having a conversation. Dramatic poems can be for a single person or for several. When more than one character speaks, it's almost like reading lines in a play. "Camp Ahoy" and "To Noises in the Night" are dramatic poems for one. "Wake-Up Call," "Going Camping," and "Shake Awake" are dramatic poems for two. "Change of Plans" and "Fishing Frenzy" are written for three voices.

EPIGRAM

An epigram is a very short poem. Often it's no more than a single couplet. It usually rhymes and has a clever ending. "Opposite of Creepy" is an epigram that's also an opposite poem.

EPIPHANY POEM

In an epiphany poem, the speaker has learned something new. The poem shows how the person's way of thinking and behaving is changing. In "Shadows Can't Grab," Lucy is learning that she has been scared of things that aren't so scary after all. Epiphany poems don't have a set structure or rhythm and rhyme pattern.

FILL-IN-THE-BLANK POEM

This form includes a simple, fun test. The poet leaves off a word at the end of the poem and the reader gets to fill in the blank. For this poem to work, it needs to rhyme or have a very strong rhythm that gives a hint about the missing word. "Bedtime in the Forest" includes the hint word *peep* so readers might be able to guess the rhyming fill-in-the-blank word *asleep*.

FOURTEENER

The fourteener gets its name from the number of syllables in each very long line. Poets usually use seven iambic feet to make up the fourteen syllables. The fourteener in poetry has been used for many centuries. "Grandpa—Pros and Cons" is a fourteener with four lines.

FREE VERSE POEM

A free verse poem is a unique form—it doesn't have
any set patterns. Poets who write free verse decide line
lengths, line breaks, the topic, and everything else.
They may use poetic techniques, rhythm, and internal
rhyme to express their thoughts. "By Lantern Light"
is a free verse poem.

HAIKU

Haiku is a poem with three lines and seventeen syllables: Five syllables
are in the first and third lines and seven syllables are in the second
line. Many centuries ago, Japanese poets wrote the first haikus. Usually in this form the subject has some connection to nature. Although
most haikus don't rhyme, "Forest Glow" does have a gentle rhyme.

HOW-TO POEM

A how-to poem is just what it sounds like—the narrator shows or tells
how to do something. In "Tent Pitching," Sam explains how to put up
a tent. "Bait Catchers" and "How to Build a Bonfire" are also how-to
poems. This type of poem could take any form and doesn't have to
rhyme.

KYRIELLE

The kyrielle is a French form that's written using quatrains. That's
a stanza with four lines. Each kyrielle line usually has eight syllables
and the fourth line in each quatrain is a repeated line (a refrain).
"Goodbye, Last Night" is a kyrielle. An example of a traditional eight-
syllable kyrielle refrain appears in it: "Goodbye, last night. Hello,
today." This poem celebrates the sunrise, so it's also an aubade.

LAMENT

A lament is a sad, serious poem. In it, the speaker expresses sorrow
or longs for something lost. This type of poem can be any length and
does not need to rhyme. "A Trick" is Lucy's lament about her mom
and dad not being able to go camping with her.

LETTER POEM

A letter poem is written in the form of a letter. This poem can be long or short and may or may not rhyme. "My Favorite Parts of Camping" is a rhyming letter poem.

LIMERICK

A limerick is a five-line rhyming poem. It has a set rhythm and rhyming pattern. The first, second, and fifth lines are longer, and their last words rhyme. The third and fourth lines are shorter and they rhyme at the end. Whether the subject is serious or lighthearted, limericks are quick and witty. "Rules for Eating S'mores" is a humorous limerick about eating a sticky dessert.

LIST POEM

A list poem is more than a random list of items. This form focuses on a specific subject and is put together with care. It may or may not rhyme and can be any length. In "Packing List," Lucy names the items the family is taking on their camping trip. "Dousing the Fire" is a list poem that's also a concrete poem.

LYRIC POEM

Long ago, lyric poems were sung to a tune played on a stringed instrument called a lyre. That's how this form was named. Lyric poems no longer need to be accompanied by music, and they don't need to rhyme. The lyric poem does have a musical, rhythmic quality. "Woodland Midnight Band" is a rhyming lyric poem that is also a serenade.

NARRATIVE POEM

In a narrative poem, the speaker describes what's happening. Often in this type of poem, the speaker isn't part of the action. In "How to Build a Bonfire," Sam narrates and also shows how a bonfire is made. A narrative poem could include rhythm and rhyme, or could be a free verse poem.

OCTAVE/OCTET

An octave is a poem or a stanza in a poem with eight lines. Poets often use couplets or quatrains to form an octave. "Stick Together" has two quatrains of four lines each to make it an octave.

OPPOSITE POEM

An opposite poem makes a contrast between two things. It's a form that was created by Richard Wilbur in the twentieth century. Opposite poems are written using rhyming couplets. They can be as many couplets long as the poet likes. In "Opposite of Creepy," Lucy describes what comforts her at bedtime. Since this poem is very short, it's also an epigram.

PARODY POEM

Writing a parody poem is a way to honor another poet. In this form, the poet chooses a few parts of an original poem to keep. The poet also decides what to change so that it's not an exact copy of the original. "Song of the Beanie Weenie Barbecue" is a parody of a chant from the play Macbeth by William Shakespeare. "Twinkle, Twinkle, Mighty Mars" is a parody of the nursery rhyme "Twinkle, Twinkle, Little Star."

POEM OF ADDRESS

A poem of address lets the speaker talk to the subject of the poem. It's usually a one-sided conversation, since the subject doesn't normally reply. In "To Noises in the Night," Lucy addresses spookiness, shadows, and strange noises. She talks to her sleeping bag in "Sleeping Bag Charm" and to the planet Mars in "Twinkle, Twinkle, Mighty Mars." A poem of address can be short or long, and may or may not rhyme.

PUN POEM

A pun is a type of wordplay where one word or phrase is substituted for another. Depending on the words used, the result can be silly or more serious. In the pun poem "Race to the Lake," Lucy says, "Three/Two/RUN," instead of "Three/Two/One."

QUATRAIN

You may already have an idea of what a quatrain is if you can count to four in a Romance language. It's a grouping of four lines. They may stand alone or be used as stanzas within longer poems. *Quatrain* comes from the French word for "four," *quatre.* "The Walls of Our Tent," "Tent Mates," and "Fishing Skills" are rhyming quatrains with different rhythm patterns and line lengths.

REPRISE POEM

A reprise poem is connected to a poem found earlier in a story. "Tear Down" is a reprise of the first *Gone Camping* poem, "Provisioning." These two poems are linked by the same three-line tercet stanza and rhythm pattern. Since the characters are different at the end of a story, the words in a reprise poem reflect those changes.

RECIPE POEM

A recipe poem lists ingredients to make something. In that way, it's a type of list poem. Recipe poems can be funny or serious and don't need to rhyme. In "Song of the Beanie Weenie Barbecue," Lucy gives ingredients and instructions for making beanie weenies.

RONDEL

A rondel is a French form with only two sets of rhymes. It usually has fourteen lines and a specific rhyme pattern. The first two lines become a refrain—they are repeated in the middle and at the end of the poem. In "Follow the Trail," the repeated lines are "One by one let's follow the trail./Hike—Two—Three—Four." Once the repeated lines are plugged in, the poet can build the rest of the poem with two quatrains. "Follow the Trail" is a rondel for two, since Lucy and Sam both speak.

RONDELET

The rondelet is related to the rondel. It also has two rhyming sounds and a refrain. It's much smaller, though, with just seven lines (a septet stanza). In "The Woods Ahead," line one is two feet long and is repeated in lines three and seven. The other four lines each have four feet. Line four rhymes with the refrain, and the remaining lines rhyme with each other.

SEPTET

A septet is a poem of seven lines. It can also be a seven-line stanza within a poem. "The Woods Ahead" is a septet with the specific rhythm and rhyme patterns that create a rondelet. Septets don't always rhyme or follow a set rhythm pattern.

SERENADE

A serenade is a song that's played outside after dark. As a poem, the words themselves are songlike and don't need a melody for the "music" to be heard. Serenades don't have to rhyme, but to work best, they need a strong rhythm. In "Woodland Midnight Band," some of the serenade music comes from the forest and the creatures living there. This is also a lyric poem.

SESTET/SEXTET

A sestet is a poem with six lines, or a six-line stanza within a bigger poem. Like other types of stanzas, the sestet doesn't have specific patterns that need to be followed. "Shore Breakfast" and "A Trick" are both sestets, but each has its own unique rhyme and rhythm pattern.

TERCET/TRIPLET

A tercet or triplet is a three-line poem or stanza. The three lines often rhyme, but it's not required. "Provisioning," "Good to Go," and "Tear Down" have rhyming tercet stanzas. "Forest Glow" is a tercet poem with the specific syllable count that makes it a haiku.

TONGUE TWISTER

Calling your poem a tongue twister gives the reader a clue that it might be tricky to read out loud. In this poem, carefully chosen sounds, words, and phrases challenge the reader to read smoothly. The faster the poem is read, the tougher it can become. A tongue twister wouldn't need to rhyme or follow a specific form to be effective. "Fishing Frenzy" is a rhyming tongue twister for three readers.

WHAT-IF

In a what-if poem, the speaker makes guesses about a situation. Using this form, the poet can exaggerate a worry or hope about something that isn't happening. This poem can take any form and may or may not rhyme. In the poem "If a Critter Creeps In," Lucy imagines the creatures that could get into the tent.

WISH POEM

In a wish poem, the speaker really wants something and makes a wish to try and get it. In "Twinkle, Twinkle, Mighty Mars," Lucy tells her wish to Mars. This is also a poem of address and a parody of the nursery rhyme "Twinkle, Twinkle, Little Star." Wish poems don't have to include a set rhythm or rhyme, and they can be on any subject.